Disney's MAIN STREET

STORYBOOK COLLECTION

Disney PRESS

New York

TABLE OF CONTENTS

TABLE OF CONTENTS

Cover design by Joe Borzetta
Interior design by Deborah Boone and Alfred Giuliani

Copyright © 2002 Disney Enterprises, Inc. All rights reserved.

"Ben and Me" story is based on the Walt Disney short film *Ben and Me*, which is based on the original story "Ben and Me" by Robert Lawson, published by Little, Brown and Company.
"Old Yeller" story is based on the Walt Disney motion picture *Old Yeller*, which is based on the novel *Old Yeller*, copyright © 1956 by Fred Gipson, published by Harper & Brothers.

Printed in the United States of America

First Edition

1 3 5 7 9 10 8 6 4 2

This book is set in 20-point Cochin.

Library of Congress Catalog Card Number: 2002101296

Disney's Americana Storybook Collection: ISBN 0-7868-3402-1

Disney's Main Street Storybook Collection: ISBN 0-7868-3431-5

For more Disney Press fun, visit www.disneybooks.com

Walt Disney's Ben and Me

If you should ever visit the fair city of Philadelphia, very likely you will see a fine statue of Benjamin Franklin—philosopher, inventor, patriot, and one of our country's first great leaders.

And if you are fortunate enough to have a good view of the crown of the statue's hat, you may see there a tiny statue of one Amos Mouse. It was Amos, you see, who was really responsible for many of the great deeds credited to Ben Franklin.

Here is the story in Amos's own words:

I was born and raised in Philadelphia, in the old church on Second Street, and, yes, I was as poor as a church mouse. There were twenty-six children in my family. Since I was the oldest, I decided to set out into the world and make my own way.

It was the winter of 1745. Jobs were scarce, especially for a mouse. All day I tramped through the snow. By nightfall, I did not know where to turn. My last hope was an old run-down shop at the edge of town. A sign over the door read BENJ. FRANKLIN, PRINTER & BOOKBINDER.

I found my way inside. The place was cold and dark and full of strange contraptions. In the shadows sat a round-faced man, trying to write by candlelight.

Suddenly, he sneezed: "Ah—*choo!*" Off flew his glasses. They crashed to the floor and broke!

"Oh, don't tell me!" cried the man, picking up his broken glasses. "My last pair! Now I'll never get this issue of my newspaper finished! It's hopeless."

"But you can't give up!" I told him. "Nothing ventured, nothing gained, Mr. Franklin!"

"My name's Ben," he said. "And who might you be?"

I introduced myself and before long, it was clear that Ben needed me around. I

helped him build a stove to warm his shop, and I fixed his glasses. He had broken both his outdoor pair and his reading pair. The only thing left to do was to make one pair out of the two.

So I fit the pieces of glass together as best I could. "Why, Amos!" he cried, when he tried them on.

"They're great! Two-way glasses! Bifocals, we'll call them." And if you know your history, of course you know that bifocals became famous.

I also helped Ben finish the latest issue of his newspaper and gave him tips to make it more interesting. By evening the next day, everyone in Philadelphia was reading it.

From then on I went everywhere with Ben, riding conveniently on his hat.

Well, the years went by, and Ben's reputation grew. Letters poured in from people all over the colonies. They asked his advice on all kinds of things. It took most of my spare time to answer them all.

Yours,

Amos

Meanwhile, Ben puttered around with his experiments. And it was one of them that led us at last to the parting of our ways. At first, he fussed around with sparks and jars with wires in them. He said he was studying electricity.

Then Ben took up kite flying. To the framework of his largest kite, he fastened a small box just for me. He said I was to be the world's first flying reporter.

I was so thrilled by flying that I failed to notice a sharp, pointed wire fastened to the kite above my head.

The first hint I had that anything was wrong was when the sky darkened with thunderclouds and a mean rain began to blow. The kite spun and shivered, but Ben would not pull me in!

I screamed myself hoarse. I tugged at the rope. Now lightning was flashing along the horizon. Thunder rolled. The storm was moving our way. Suddenly, lightning struck my kite! The shock went through me and almost tore the kite to ribbons.

Now—too late—Ben began to wind in his rope. The kite and I slowly descended and landed in a tree. When Ben found us there, he scooped me up in one hand.

"Amos! Amos! Speak to me!" he cried. "Was it electricity?"

I couldn't believe it! All he cared about was whether or not the sizzle in a lightning bolt was the same as electricity! That was the end for me!

"Good-bye, forever!" I said. He pleaded with me to change my mind, but I left Ben and went back to my family in the old church.

The years that followed were troubled ones. Restless crowds filled the streets. There were riots as well as loud talk against the stamp tax and other taxes for the British king. Ben was chosen to go to England and lay our case before the king.

The colonies eagerly awaited his return. But his mission was a failure. The king would not listen. It seemed as if war would surely come. But the people had no clear statement of their cause to hold them together. I heard that poor Ben was worried.

I could help him — I knew I could. But no! I could not go back. After all, a mouse has his pride!

Then, one night in 1776, I was awakened by a voice. Sleepily, I peered through the mouse hole. There, on bended knee, was Ben Franklin himself.

"Amos, I'm here to ask you to come back," he said humbly.

I was pleased and touched, but I did not let him see it.

"I have big decisions to make," Ben continued, "and I can't make them alone. You just must come back."

"On my own terms?" I asked. "If I draw up an agreement, will you sign it?"

"I'll sign anything," he vowed.

So back I went, having spent the night writing the agreement by candlelight.

Ben was glad to see me the next morning, you may be sure. I gave him my agreement to sign at once.

That was
when a knock
came at the
door. It was
Thomas
Jefferson. He
was one of
the leaders of

the colonies, too, and Ben called him "Red." He was
writing a statement about what the colonists believed
in—a Declaration of Independence.

But, struggle as he would, Red could not get the beginning right.

"'The time has come—'" Red began to read, but then he stopped. "No, Ben, it isn't right. 'The time is at hand' . . . no . . . ."

"Psst, Ben!" I said, when I saw how upset Red was. "How about our contract?"

"Shh!" said Ben. "Just a minute."

"No," I insisted. "Now!"

So Ben began to read the contract aloud: "'When in the course of human events, it becomes necessary—'"

"Ben!" cried Red Jefferson. "That's it! That's it!"

So that's how it happened that I supplied the beginning for the Declaration of Independence. Oh, I didn't get credit, of course. But fame doesn't matter to a mouse. I have my memories of the good old days and Ben and me.

Walt Disney's

GOOFY, Movie Star

Once upon a time there was a wonderful place called Hollywood. It was the center of Movie Land.

Everyone in Hollywood, it seemed, wanted to be a movie star.

Every waitress
was waiting to be
discovered so she
could be a movie
star. And every
young man working
in a filling station
planned to be one,

too. They were all waiting for a talent scout to come
along and change their lives. For a talent scout, you
know, is a person who finds new movie stars.

Driving down the streets of Hollywood, you knew at once you were in Movie Land. You almost wanted to be a movie star yourself.

There was just one person in Hollywood, it seemed, who didn't care to be a movie star. His name was Dippy Dog, and he was a happy soul.

Dippy liked the movies, of course. He liked to sit in the balcony of the theater with some popcorn and see a picture show.

"*Yuk, yuk, yuk!*" He would laugh his merry laugh. And everyone around would laugh with him.

One night at the movie theater, some talent scouts heard Dippy laugh. "Who is that laughing?" they cried. "He has the makings of a movie star!" And when they found out it was Dippy Dog, the talent scouts hustled him off to a movie studio.

Soon Dippy was about to sign a contract to be a movie star.

"What's your name, son?" asked the producer.

"Dippy Dog? That will never do! We need a name that breathes romance: Dandy—Daffy—*Goofy*! That's it!"

So Goofy signed his new name to the contract. And then he was a movie star.

Now Goofy had to dress like a movie star. He had whole closets full of fancy clothes.

And he had to have some shiny new cars—not just one new car, but four!

He had to move from his little house to a mansion worthy of a star.

And Goofy had to have his picture taken, of course. He had

his picture taken waking up, eating his breakfast—even brushing his teeth.

He had his picture taken dressed for golf and tennis and hopscotch and polo.

Goofy was so busy having pictures taken for newspapers and magazines and television shows that he had to make a special appointment to play.

He even had pictures taken for a movie. He was the

star, of course.

Now whenever he went to eat in a restaurant, movie

fans waited at the door to see him walk in and out.

The night his movie opened, all the pretty girls and handsome young men who wanted to be movie stars also lined up outside the theater.

"Isn't he wonderful?" they said. "How did he do it?"

Then along came a famous newspaper writer to interview the new star. "What is the secret of your success?" she asked.

"*Yuk, yuk, yuk!*" Goofy laughed the laugh that made him famous. "I guess I just have fun, that's all."

And that is the story of how Goofy became a movie star in Hollywood, once upon a time.

DUMBO

It was spring—
spring in the circus!
After the long winter's
rest, it was time to
set out again on the
open road.

"Toot! Toot!"
whistled Casey Jones,
the locomotive of the
circus train, and the
circus was on its way!

Inside the elephant car, a stork had just delivered Mrs. Jumbo's baby. And a darling baby elephant he was, too. One of the grown-up elephants tickled him under his chin. The tickling made him sneeze. And when he sneezed, out flapped his ears — the most enormous ears any of them had ever seen!

All the grown-up elephants laughed. "He'll never be a Little Jumbo," they said. "Little *Dumbo* is the name for him!"

Poor little Dumbo toddled to his mother, and she tenderly rocked him to sleep.

Before dawn, Casey Jones brought the train to

a stop in the city where the circus was to open. After

the tents were set up, there was a big parade down

the main street: horses, acrobats, lions in their

wagon-cages, and, last but not least, the elephants

marching slowly in single file.

At the end of the line came Dumbo, and all went well until the crowd caught sight of his ears.

"He can't be an elephant!" they cried. "He must be a clown!"

Dumbo tried
to walk faster. But
he stumbled and
tripped on his
ears. Down he
went in a puddle
of mud. The

crowd roared with laughter.

Later, at the circus grounds, some boys gathered in
front of Dumbo and Mrs. Jumbo. One boy grabbed
Dumbo's ear and pulled it—hard.

Mrs. Jumbo would not stand for that! She snatched the boy up with her trunk, dropped him across the rope, and spanked him.

"Help, help!" cried the boy, and the keepers came running. Soon Mrs. Jumbo was behind bars in the prison wagon with a big sign that said DANGER! MAD ELEPHANT!

Poor Dumbo. He missed his mother, and the other elephants would have nothing to do with him. Little Timothy, the circus mouse, was his only friend. Timothy wanted to help Dumbo find a special use for those special ears and become famous!

Timothy helped
Dumbo practice
springboard
jumping so that
he could jump
atop the pyramid
of elephants at
the end of the
show. But when

the big moment came, Dumbo tripped over his ears
and knocked over the elephant pyramid.

That did it. The next day, they made Dumbo into a clown. He had to jump from the top of a blazing cardboard house, down into the clown-firemen's net.

But Timothy would not give up. "We'll have you starring yet," Timothy whispered to Dumbo. "You'll be flying high."

Back in the

circus tent,

with Timothy

curled up in

his hat brim,

Dumbo drifted

off to sleep and

dreamed a beautiful dream. In it, he was the star of a

magical circus. He stepped onto a springboard, bounced

high into the air—and then away he flew.

It seemed as easy as anything, and very, very real.

The next morning, Timothy was the first to awaken. He was still in the brim of Dumbo's hat, and the hat was still on Dumbo's head. But Dumbo was asleep on the branch of a tree, far above the ground!

"You and that elephant just came flying up," some crows said to Timothy.

"Flying?" yelled Timothy.

Dumbo opened his eyes, tried to stand up, and fell out of the tree.

"Dumbo!" cried Timothy. "If you can fly when you're asleep, you can fly when you're awake." So Dumbo tried again . . . and again. . . . But he could not leave the ground.

At last the crows felt sorry for him. "Here, try this magic feather," one of them said. "Hold on to this, and you'll be fine."

Dumbo clutched the feather in his trunk and tried

once more. It

worked! Up

into the air he

soared like a

bird. He glided,

he dipped, he dove. The crows cheered.

Timothy cheered, too, as he and Dumbo headed

back to the circus grounds. They decided to keep

Dumbo's flying a secret — a surprise for the afternoon

show.

So Dumbo and Timothy waited inside the cardboard house all through the show, until the make-believe fire crackled up around them. Then Timothy tucked the magic feather into Dumbo's trunk, and climbed into Dumbo's hat brim.

Down below, the clown-firemen brought a big net, held it out, and Dumbo jumped!

But as he jumped, the feather slipped from his trunk. Now his magic was gone, Dumbo thought. He began to plunge like a stone.

Timothy saw the feather drift away. Thinking quickly, he shouted, "The feather was a trick! You can fly by yourself!"

Doubtfully, Dumbo spread his ears wide—and swooped up into the air!

The audience roared with delight. Dumbo was flying!

In that instant, everything changed for Dumbo. The keepers freed Mrs. Jumbo and brought her into the tent to see her baby fly. Soon Dumbo was a

hero from coast to coast. Timothy became his manager and saw to it that Dumbo got a wonderful contract with a big salary and a pension for his mother.

And the circus was even renamed "Dumbo's Flying Circus" in honor of the elephant with the very special ears and a very special talent.

* * * ⭐ * * *

Down Texas way, the Pecos River flows. Where it comes from, no one knows!

One day, a long time back, when a prairie wagon full of children, dogs, pots, and pans was crossing the Pecos River, the smallest child just rolled right out the back!

That child's name was Bill. He sat there all alone on the prairie until a mother coyote came along and took pity on him. She decided to take him home and raise him as her own, along with her coyote pups.

Bill felt right at home with the coyotes — and with all the other animals out on the prairie. He was spunky, too. As Bill grew, he learned how to out-lope the antelopes, out-jump the jackrabbits, and out-hiss the snakes!

Then one day, a young colt wandered into the Pecos

land. The poor thing was weak and couldn't defend himself against the buzzards. So Bill decided to help him out. Before long, Bill had taken care of those buzzards, and Bill and the colt were friends.

From then on, those two stuck together like warts

on a toad. As Bill grew, he became a cowboy—the

"toughest critter west of the Alamo!" His weak, little

colt grew into a big, strong horse known as Widowmaker,

because he had bucked off so many cowboys.

Why, the two of them became famous in the Pecos

land, and

their deeds

even more

so. Bill

could rope

anything

with his

lariat—

even a raging cyclone. He straddled it, then tamed it to a breeze.

When there was a drought all over Texas, Bill lassoed

and towed a rain cloud from California to wet things down. That's how we got the Gulf of Mexico!

And when a group of cattle rustlers stole Bill's herd, he caught the villains and knocked out all their fillings. That's the reason we have gold in them thar hills!

Once, Bill lost his way in the desert. He knew he'd

never make it across without some water. So he got a

stick and dug the Rio Grande as he went!

Through it all, Widowmaker was always at Bill's

side. It looked as though nothing would ever come

between Bill

and his horse.

Then along

came Sluefoot

Sue, the first

woman Bill

had ever seen.

To Widowmaker, Sue looked like trouble. And sure enough, she was, for Bill and Sue soon fell in love.

Sue wanted to marry Bill, and she wanted to do it while riding Widowmaker. Well, that

horse was not about to stand for it. The cowhands brought him over to her, fit to be tied! That didn't bother Sue. She climbed right on Widowmaker's back.

The more that horse bucked and reared, the tighter she

 hung on. She was a

real bronc rider!

The only

problem was that

Sue was wearing a

wire bustle under

her wedding dress.

Little by little, that bustle began to act as a spring as she

bounced up and down, each time sending her higher

and higher into the air.

Then, suddenly, the reins snapped and Sue went flying skyward!

Well, Bill got out his lariat and swung it in a wide loop. Hadn't he lassoed everything from a cyclone to a gang of rustlers? Surely, he could lasso Sue and bring her back down to earth.

He threw the loop wide and high up in the sky. But for the first time in his life . . . Bill missed. No one could understand it, except Widowmaker. He was standing on the rope!

Sue kept on flying right up to the moon,

and that was where she stayed for all time. As for Bill,

he rode away from the plains and never returned.

Folks think he went back to the coyotes. They say

that when the coyotes howl at the full moon, you can

hear Bill howling right along with them.

But just ask anyone today who the best cowboy in Texas is. They'll still tell you it's Pecos Bill!

"I've had such fun today, Mickey!" exclaimed Minnie Mouse. "There's so much to do here at Walt Disney World—the rides, the shops, the movies . . . and, of course, the yummy snacks!"

"I had fun, too," Mickey said. "And I can't wait to lead the parade tonight! I'll get to wear my brand-new drum major's hat. I have it right—oh, no!"

Mickey's hat was missing!

"I had it with me all day," said Mickey. "I must have left it someplace."

"I'll help you look for it," Minnie said. "Come on. Our last stop was Space Mountain," she added as they headed back to the ride.

Mickey and Minnie held on as the ride swooped around high-speed curves. "Wow! What a ride!" said Mickey. "But I don't see my hat."

Mickey and Minnie found their friend Donald Duck at their next stop—the Grand Prix Raceway.

"I haven't seen your hat," Donald said as he sped away. "But I just saw Goofy, and he was wearing a new hat."

Mickey and Minnie searched all over Tomorrowland for the missing hat. "Let's catch the Skyway," Minnie suggested.

Soon they were floating high above Fantasyland. As they scanned the park below, it seemed to Mickey that everyone had a hat on. But he didn't see his own.

They bumped into Daisy Duck at It's a Small World and told her about the missing hat.

"I haven't seen it," Daisy said, "but I heard Goofy got a new hat today."

"Hmm," said Mickey. "That's what Donald said."

"Next stop, Frontierland," Minnie said.

"Gee, it would be fun to take a riverboat ride,"
Mickey said.

"We'll do that

next time!" said

Minnie. "For now,

we had better

check out Big

Thunder Mountain

Railroad." But

there was no sign of the hat there, either.

Minnie tried to reassure Mickey. "Don't worry," she said. "We'll find your hat." When they reached Liberty Square, Mickey spotted a hat outside the Hall of Presidents. But it turned out to be Ben Franklin's, not Mickey's.

Before long, the search led Mickey and Minnie to the Pirates of the Caribbean ride in Adventureland, where they met up with Huey, Dewey, and Louie.

"Hi, boys," Mickey said. "Have you seen my new drum major's hat? I lost it somewhere in the Magic Kingdom."

"Nope," said Huey.

"But Goofy has a new hat," added Dewey.

"Yeah, it's really cool," finished Louie.

On the Jungle Cruise, Mickey began to wonder if he would *ever* find his new hat.

Minnie giggled. "I sure hope the hippos didn't eat it!" she said.

"Gosh, Minnie," said Mickey, as they passed Cinderella Castle. "Where could that hat be? I just can't lead the parade without it!"

"I know we'll find it, Mickey. We still haven't checked Main Street, U.S.A.," Minnie reminded him.

Mickey and Minnie went from shop to shop on Main Street. They still couldn't find Mickey's hat anywhere. Mickey was ready to give up his search. But there was one more place to look—the movie theater.

Just then, they spotted their friend, Goofy. He was carrying a *very* familiar object.

"My hat!" Mickey cried.

"It's yours?" Goofy exclaimed. "*Gawrsh*, I had no idea. I found it in the movie theater."

Mickey had found his hat just in time. He wore it proudly as he marched in the big parade. It was the perfect ending to another wonderful day at Walt Disney World.

Walt Disney's

Paul Revere

There once was a man named Paul Revere who went riding under the midnight moon for liberty, because he wanted a country without a king.

Who was this Paul Revere?

Paul Revere was a silversmith in old Boston town. If anything could be made of silver, Paul Revere could make it. In his shop on Fish Street, he made teapots and cream pots, buckles and bowls, and spoons and jugs and cups.

One April night, he left his shop and walked quickly through the streets, keeping away from the king's soldiers in their red coats. He soon met up with a man named Robert Newman.

"The king's soldiers march tonight," Paul Revere said. "They want to capture two of our men. I am riding to Lexington to give the warning."

Robert Newman nodded. "I know the plan. I will show lanterns from the

church tower to tell our men how the British go: one if by land, and two if by sea."

"Show two lanterns," said Paul Revere. "The redcoats are going by sea."

While Robert Newman started up the tower, Paul Revere hurried home. He put on his boots and riding coat and said good-bye to his wife and children. To his oldest son, he said, "Now it's up to you to take care of things, for there's no telling if I will return."

Once again, Paul Revere went out into the night. With two friends, he headed to the riverbank where he had hidden a rowboat.

"My spurs!" he said. "I've forgotten them! How can I ride without them?"

Then he saw that his dog had followed him. He wrote a note to Mrs. Revere and tied it to the dog's collar.

"Home, boy!" he said. "Home—as fast as you can!"

The dog was back in a few minutes, and tied around his neck were the spurs.

Getting into the boat, Paul Revere and his friends began to row across the river. To reach Lexington, Paul Revere first had to sneak past the *Somerset*, one of the king's big ships. At any moment, Paul Revere expected to hear cannon fire or the shout of a ship's officer. But none came, and at last the rowboat touched shore.

Not far from shore, Paul Revere met some men. They led him to the house of Deacon John Larkin, a friend of Paul Revere's, and gave him a horse.

"You must be careful, sir," said one of the men. "There are redcoats on the road."

Then Paul Revere began riding, riding, riding for liberty. Past fields and meadows, past orchards and farms, he rode toward Lexington.

Suddenly, ahead of him, he saw two men on horseback. Their pistols gleamed in the moonlight. Redcoats!

One of the soldiers galloped toward him, and Paul Revere cut across a field. Near a swamp he suddenly turned aside. He smiled as the horse behind him crashed into the swamp, its hooves sinking into the mud.

Spurring his horse on, Paul Revere raced to another road. Riding, riding, riding, he came at last to Lexington. He warned Sam Adams and John Hancock that the soldiers were coming for them.

Then Paul Revere continued riding toward the village of Concord. At every house along the way, he shouted: "To arms! To arms! The redcoats are coming!"

Everywhere men reached for their rifles. Church bells rang, and drums rolled— for the redcoats were coming, and the time had arrived to fight for liberty.

The war went on for years. And when it was over, there was a new country—the United States of America. It was a country without a king, just as Paul Revere had wanted.

And Americans have never forgotten Paul Revere,

who rode for liberty under the midnight moon.

Walt Disney's
Pluto Pup
Goes to Sea

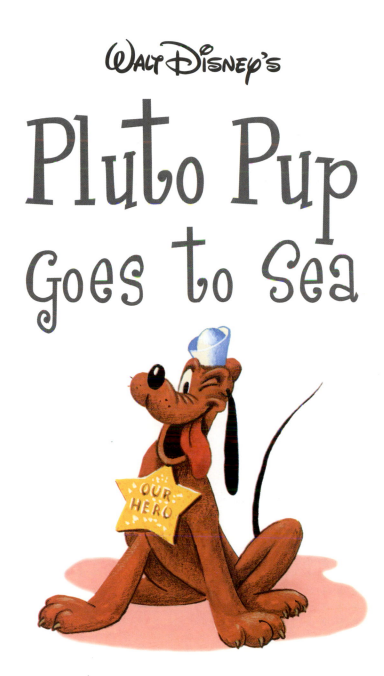

"You see that dog up there? That dog's a hero!" Mickey Mouse told Pluto Pup one day. They were down at the town dock, standing beside an ocean liner. Up on the deck lay a huge dog, looking proud and staring out to sea.

"There was a story in the paper about all the lives he's saved," said Mickey. "Wouldn't it be swell if you were a dog like that?"

Pluto thought, if all you had to do to be a hero was lie on a deck, staring out to sea, then he was willing to try it. The next gangplank they came to, up Pluto went.

Mickey did not miss him for a few minutes. Then he whistled and called and looked all around. But he could not find Pluto. High above, on the deck of a sleek white yacht, Pluto was sitting all alone, looking proud and haughty, and gazing out to sea.

No one on the yacht knew Pluto was on board until they had left the harbor for the open sea. Then the waves rose and fell, the yacht pitched and tossed, and Pluto was as unhappy as a dog can be.

Down below, the sailors shuddered at the dismal moans that came from the deck above. When they checked, they soon found the stowaway and led him to

a corner of the hold where they made him a bed of old rags.

"Too bad he doesn't

have sea legs,"
said the second
mate to the
first. "We
could use
a smart
watchdog for
the captain's
jewels."

"Shh!" The first mate put a finger to his lips. "No
one must know about those jewels!"

But it was too late. A tough-looking sailor had overheard the whole thing.

"Aha!" he said to himself. "Them jewels will line my pockets soon, and I'll jump ship at the very first port, or my name's not Pegleg Pete!"

The next day, Pluto felt much better. His nose led

him to the
galley, where the
ship's cat lived
with the cook.
Pluto heard the
cat hiss and he
took off for the
deck. The cat
came racing after

him so fast that, as the ship lurched, she slid across the

deck, under the rail, and down into the sea!

Pluto ran over for a better look—and skidded, with a yelp, right after her!

After the sailors rescued them, they decided that Pluto had jumped in to save the cat. They called him a hero and moved his bed to the captain's cabin.

"He's just the dog we need to guard the captain's jewels, after all," they said.

Pluto did not like being shut up in the cabin, though. He sent up such a howl that night that the captain shouted for the mates. "Take that mutt away. I'd rather be guarded *from* him than *by* him!" he cried.

So Pluto went back to his first spot on deck, looking proudly out to sea. He kept a sharp eye out for anyone about to fall overboard, because he liked the life of a hero.

That was the

night Pegleg

Pete had picked

to steal the

captain's jewels.

The ship lay

close to shore,

and Pete had

arranged for his friends to meet him with a boat. So

Pete slipped down to the cabin where the captain was

sound asleep and stole the jewels.

With the jewels safely stowed in a small leather pouch, Pegleg Pete signaled to his friends onshore. When they signaled back, he kicked off his shoe, and

dove over the rail into the water below. *Splash!* He started to swim for shore.

But Pluto had
heard the splash.
One of his friends
must have fallen
overboard, he
thought. Time to
be a hero again!

So Pluto jumped into the water, too.

"Man overboard!" the lookout yelled. The sailors
turned the searchlight on and soon picked up Pluto and
Pegleg Pete, bobbing in the water below.

Back on board, Pete quickly made up a story. "I saw the dear mutt slide in," he claimed. "I couldn't bear to think of anything happening to him, so I jumped in to save him, of course."

"Is that so?" said the first mate. "Then you won't mind showing me what's in that pouch!"

"I'll go get the captain!" the second mate cried, and ran off.

Pegleg Pete knew he was in big trouble. "Let me go!" he shouted, and he ran for the rail.

But Pluto did not want another bath in that cold water! He made a frantic jump for Pete's trousers and hung on to them!

Soon the second mate was back with the captain.

"Put Pete in the brig," the captain said. "And we'll get *you* a medal, sir," he said to Pluto the Pup.

So when the yacht came home at last, with Pluto sitting proudly up on deck, he was wearing the biggest, shiniest medal to be had. OUR HERO it said in gold.

Mickey was wandering down by the docks, as he did every lonely day, looking for his lost pup, when the yacht came into port.

"Arf!" cried Pluto, when he spotted Mickey.

"Pluto!" cried Mickey. "Where have you been? And look at that medal! What does it mean?"

The sailors told Mickey the whole tale.

"I guess you won't want to come back home, now that you're a ship's hero," Mickey said sadly.

In answer, Pluto gnawed his medal off his collar and laid it at Mickey's feet. He still thought the finest thing of all was to be Mickey Mouse's dog!

Walt Disney's
Paul Bunyan

Early one morning after a ferocious storm, a huge cradle washed up near a town in Maine. Inside the cradle was the biggest baby anyone had ever seen.

The townsfolk adopted him and named him Paul Bunyan, because they thought it sounded like a big guy's name!

Paul grew into a good lad and everybody liked him.

He went to school just like all the other kids, but he was too big to fit inside the classroom.

So he sat outside and handed his lessons to the teacher by lifting the roof.

When school let out, all the kids would head for the old swimming hole. For huge Paul, it was more like a bathtub.

Paul was interested in a lot of things as a youngster. But as he got older and even bigger, he spent

more and more time out in the woods watching the loggers cut down trees. They cleared land so that farmers could plant crops, and they used the lumber to build new homes.

Babe became Paul's closest friend, and he was mighty strong, too. One time, Paul set up a logging

camp near a river that had too many bends in it for logs to float down. So Paul tied one end of a rope to Babe's yoke and anchored the other end in the river.

Babe pulled that river straight as a pine log!

Paul and
Babe kept
moving
westward.
As they
passed

through Minnesota, they got lost in a rainstorm. They

wandered in circles for days. The big puddles left by

their footprints remained full of water, and to this day

folks still call Minnesota "the land of ten thousand

lakes."

By summer's end, Paul and Babe had reached Wyoming. They were so glad to finally be out west that they got into a friendly wrestling match. They kicked up a whole mountain range, which is now called the Grand Tetons.

Out west, among the giant trees, there were big

logging camps that were just the kind of places for

Paul. Paul and Babe fit right in, with their hard work

and hearty appetites.

Then one day, a

stranger rolled into

camp aboard a shiny

new locomotive.

He walked right

up to a tree and began to cut it with a machine, the

likes of which no logger had ever seen!

"My name," said the stranger, "is Joe Muffaw, and I've got an automatic tree-cutting machine and a log-pulling locomotive that'll do your work in half the time."

Paul was angry. "Out here we use a double-bladed ax for cutting and oxen for pulling, little fella," he said.

Before long, a contest was organized to see who

could pull a triple load of logs faster: the locomotive or Babe the Blue Ox. Babe and the locomotive pulled with all their might, snorting and puffing. But when it was over, Babe had lost by just half an inch.

Sadly, Paul and Babe decided to say "so long" to their friends and head north.

Whatever happened to Paul Bunyan and Babe? Some folks say that logging machines put Paul out of business.

But others say that Paul went to Alaska, where the logging is endless and a man and his ox still have plenty of room.

Walt Disney's

Old Yeller

Nobody knew where Old Yeller came from. He just turned up one day at the Coateses' cabin, sniffing and snuffing and wagging his tail.

The Coates boys, Arliss and Travis, looked him over. Not that he was much to look at. He was big and clumsy and yellow in color.

He was full
of tricks, too.
Whenever
anyone picked
up a stick or a
stone, Old
Yeller threw
himself on the
ground. He
rolled around,
howling and yowling worse than a wildcat.

And he had to be watched. If he wasn't, he'd steal a person blind. Why, he could snatch a whole side of meat as slick as you please.

Old Yeller and Arliss took to each other right off. But Mrs. Coates wasn't sure if they should keep the dog. "If

your papa was here, he'd know what to do," she said.

But Mr. Coates was miles away, selling their steers in Abilene. He wouldn't be back for months. So Mrs. Coates told Arliss that Old Yeller could stay for the time being.

Whooping and hollering, Arliss ran for the pond, with Old Yeller right behind him.

Standing still, Old Yeller looked as though he couldn't walk without falling over his own feet. But when he started running, he was like a streak of lightning greased with hot bear oil. He was swift and sure and a sight to see.

He was so fast that he once caught a good-sized catfish in the pond for Arliss. Another time, he helped Travis drive some thieving raccoons out of the corn patch. And he was a wonder at herding cows or hogs.

Then one day, Arliss did something he shouldn't have and got himself into real trouble. He caught a bear cub

by the leg. And he wouldn't let go, not even when the big old mother bear came charging at him, snarling and growling.

Suddenly, from no place in particular, Old Yeller came bounding up. He tore right into that old bear.

And while Old Yeller fought the bear, Mrs. Coates and Travis came running and pulled Arliss away from the cub.

Soon the big
bear had enough of
the fighting and
was running off
through the brush
with her cub. After
he saw that Arliss
was safe, Old Yeller
wagged his tail.

"Oh, you crazy, wonderful old dog!" Mrs. Coates
said. Now she was certain Old Yeller should stay.

But a few days later, a man came riding up to the cabin. His name was Sanderson, and he had lost a dog—a big yellow dog that was full of tricks. Old Yeller was his.

When Mr. Sanderson started to take Old Yeller away, Arliss shouted, "You can't have my dog!" Mrs. Coates and Travis had to hold him back.

Mr. Sanderson looked at Arliss and then got down from his horse.

"Just a minute, young fellow," he said. "What's that in your pocket?"

"A horned toad," Arliss said, and held it out.

"Finest horned toad I ever saw," Mr. Sanderson said. Then, right then and there, Mr. Sanderson offered to swap his dog for Arliss's toad . . . if Mrs. Coates threw in a good home-cooked meal. Mrs. Coates smiled and nodded.

"All right. It's a swap," Mr. Sanderson said.

And so, Mr. Sanderson got a toad and a meal—and Arliss got Old Yeller.

"You're really my dog now, aren't you, boy?" Arliss said.

Old Yeller just wagged his tail and lay down in front of the fire. He knew he was there to stay.

Walt Disney's
Casey at the Bat

The outlook wasn't brilliant for the Mudville nine that day:

The score stood four to two with but one inning more to play.

And then when Cooney died at first, and Barrows did the same,

A sickly silence fell upon the patrons of the game.

A straggling few got up to go in deep despair. The rest

Clung to that hope which springs eternal in the human breast;

They thought if only Casey could but get a whack at that—

We'd put up even money now, with Casey at the bat.

But Flynn preceded Casey, as did also Jimmy Blake,

And the former was a lulu and the latter was a cake;

So upon that stricken multitude grim melancholy sat,

For there seemed but little chance of Casey's getting to the bat.

But Flynn let drive a single, to the wonderment of all,

And Blake, the much despis-ed, tore the cover off the ball;

And when the dust had lifted, and the men saw what had occurred,

There was Jimmy safe at second and Flynn a-hugging third.

Then from five thousand throats and more there rose a lusty yell;

It rumbled through the valley, it rattled in the dell;

It knocked upon the mountain and recoiled upon the flat,

For Casey, mighty Casey, was advancing to the bat.

There was ease in Casey's manner as he stepped into his place;

There was pride in Casey's bearing and a smile on Casey's face.

And when, responding to the cheers, he lightly doffed his hat,

No stranger in the crowd could doubt 'twas Casey at the bat.

Ten thousand eyes were on him as he rubbed his hands with dirt;

Five thousand tongues applauded when he wiped them on his shirt.

Then while the writhing pitcher ground the ball into his hip,

Defiance gleamed in Casey's eye, a sneer curled Casey's lip.

And now the leather-covered sphere came hurtling through the air,

And Casey stood a-watching it in haughty grandeur there.

Close by the sturdy batsman the ball unheeded sped—

"That ain't my style," said Casey. "Strike one," the umpire said.

From the benches, black with people, there went up a muffled roar,

Like the beating of the storm-waves on a stern and distant shore.

"Kill him! Kill the umpire!" shouted someone on the stand;

And it's likely they'd have killed him had not Casey raised his hand.

With a smile of Christian charity great Casey's visage shone;

He stilled the rising tumult; he bade the game go on;

He signaled to the pitcher, and once more the spheroid flew;

But Casey still ignored it, and the umpire said, "Strike two."

"Fraud!" cried the maddened thousands, and echo answered fraud;

But one scornful look from Casey and the audience was awed.

They saw his face grow stern and cold, they saw his muscles strain,

And they knew that Casey wouldn't let that ball go by again.

The sneer is gone from Casey's lip, his teeth are clenched in hate;

He pounds with cruel violence his bat upon the plate.

And now the pitcher holds the ball, and now he lets it go,

And now the air is shattered by the force of Casey's blow.

Oh, somewhere in this favored land the sun is shining bright;

The band is playing somewhere, and somewhere hearts are light;

And somewhere men are laughing, and somewhere children shout;

But there is no joy in Mudville—mighty Casey has struck out.

Walt Disney's
The Ugly Dachshund

The Garrisons had three little dachshund pups—
Chloe, Heidi, and Wilhelma—who were the
favorites of Mrs. Garrison. And they had a fourth pup,
who was the
favorite of Mr.
Garrison. His
name was
Brutus and he
was a Great
Dane. Poor Brutus! He thought he was a dachshund,
too—a very large, clumsy, ugly dachshund.

Brutus grew and grew, as Great Dane pups always do. Soon, when Brutus stood on his hind legs, he was almost as tall as Mrs. Garrison. But he kept on thinking that he was a dachshund. He even ran the way dachshunds do—low and close to the ground.

Chloe, Heidi, and Wilhelma pattered into the house one day. Chloe grabbed a ball of wool in her mouth and ran. Heidi and Wilhelma chased her. Big Brutus lumbered after them, trying to join in the fun.

The ball unwound, and soon there was nothing but a mass of tangled wool.

The three dachshunds scampered off. But before poor Brutus could follow them, in came Mrs. Garrison.

"Brutus!" she cried. "Look at what you've done!"

Another day, the three little dachshunds and Brutus raced into Mr. Garrison's art studio. Brutus knocked down a jar of paintbrushes, backed into a cabinet, and crashed into an enormous easel. When Mr. Garrison scolded him, poor Brutus whimpered sadly.

"Well, he's done it again," said Mrs. Garrison.

"Yes," said Mr. Garrison, "but after all, he's just a puppy."

"That's what worries me," said Mrs. Garrison. "What will he do when he gets bigger?"

Finally, Mr. Garrison was forced to put Brutus in an outdoor pen. After several whimpers, the pup settled down and closed his eyes.

Hours later, Brutus's eyes suddenly snapped open and he growled. Rising, he began to paw at the sides of the pen.

In the darkness, a strange man was coming toward the house. Brutus charged. In one big jump, he was out of the pen.

With a flying leap, he knocked down the stranger.

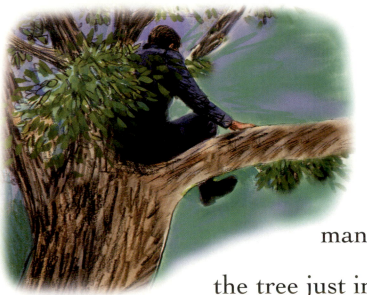

The stranger jumped to his feet and headed for a tree, with Brutus right behind him. The man swung himself up into the tree just in time. Brutus circled below, barking loudly.

Inside the house, the Garrisons thought that Brutus was barking because he was lonely. They turned over and went back to sleep.

Poor Brutus. It turned out that the strange man was a policeman who had been looking for prowlers. The Garrisons were sorry that the policeman had spent all night up in the tree. But Mr. Garrison was delighted that Brutus was such a good watchdog.

So Brutus stayed on with the Garrisons and the dachshunds. Before long, Brutus was no longer an oversized pup. He was a full-grown Great Dane—but he still thought he was a dachshund.

One night, the Garrisons had a party. Brutus was not invited. He was supposed to spend the evening in the backyard. Mrs. Garrison proudly showed Chloe to a guest. "She never gets into trouble the way Brutus does," she said.

Suddenly, there was an unexpected guest at the party! Brutus had managed to loosen his leash. Barking his friendliest barks, he came galloping among the guests. Chairs were soon knocked over, tables were toppled, and the guests scattered. The party was over.

Brutus was in disgrace. Even Mr. Garrison agreed that something had to be done. But the very next day, Brutus redeemed himself. Chloe fell into the garbage can. When the garbage man came and emptied the trash — and Chloe — into

his truck, Brutus barked and barked until the Garrisons came out to rescue the little dachshund.

From then on, Mrs. Garrison no longer complained about Brutus, but she still thought he was a clumsy ox of a dog. So Mr. Garrison entered Brutus in an upcoming dog show. With the help of Doc Pruitt, a friendly kennel owner, Mr. Garrison taught Brutus to heel and stay. But there was still one thing Doc Pruitt couldn't figure out: "Why does he droop that way in the middle?" he asked.

"He still thinks he's a dachshund," Mr. Garrison said gloomily.

The day of the dog show soon arrived. When the Great Danes were called up, Mr. Garrison swallowed hard and led Brutus to the showring. And there, for the first time ever, Brutus saw other Great Danes! How tall and strong they were! How very handsome!

Brutus eyed the other Danes. Suddenly, he lifted his head proudly. At last he knew he was a Great Dane!

And can you guess which Great Dane won first prize that day. . . ?

It was Brutus! Mrs. Garrison was surprised and delighted.

There are still three little dachshunds living with the Garrisons. And with them lives a fourth dog of whom they're very proud. He is a huge and handsome Great Dane, and Brutus is his name.

Even when the road of life gets rocky, every heart has a way to make its dream come true. And that's exactly what John Henry believed. In fact, John Henry believed it so strongly that he laid down his very life for his dream.

John Henry and his dearest love, Polly, were born slaves. They didn't have a single thing to call their own. But all that changed when President Abraham Lincoln signed the Emancipation Proclamation, which freed all the slaves.

That's when John Henry vowed never to let his soul be chained again. He and Polly were married, and as a wedding present to her new husband, Polly had his slave chains forged into a mighty hammer. Then they set off together to find work and a place of their own.

In Talcott, West Virginia, John and Polly came upon a crew of workers laying new train track for the C&O Railroad. The railroad had promised fifty acres of land to every man who helped finish the line.

It was backbreaking work. It took the strength of three men to hammer in every steel spike that held the new track in place. To make matters worse, the railroad had moved up the crew's deadline.

"If we do not get to the other side of that mountain," said the foreman, "we can kiss our land good-bye!"

The workers were outraged. But John Henry confidently stepped forward with his hammer in his hand. "I'll take you there," he said, and he drove a spike into the ground with a single blow of his hammer.

The men looked on in amazement as John Henry went right to work, hammering in spike after spike,

 while Polly began to sing a work song to set the rhythm of their pace. The other men picked up their hammers and followed John's lead. Their spirits were lifted and their pace quickened.

As the work went on and the sound of John's hammer rang out, he met every challenge. John was an incredibly strong man. He could arm wrestle three men at once and beat them handily. He could drive a spike into a rock wall like a knife through butter.

Catching John Henry's spirit, the crew was soon back on schedule. The men felt that the dream of owning their own land was truly within their grasp. They took a break from their work to look down at the valley that would be their home when the job was done.

Then one morning, the crew's work was interrupted.
The ground vibrated as a large machine emerged from
a cloud of steam and came rolling up to the work site.
Workers scattered, but John stood to face the machine
as it rolled to a halt.

At that, the angry workers charged the machine and tried to topple it. But John knew that wouldn't solve anything. He had an idea—a better way to settle things. He issued a challenge to the steam-drill driver: "I've got two free hands and a twenty-pound hammer. If I can beat this here machine, the land you promised is ours."

The driver tipped his hat in agreement, and the race was set to begin at once.

Polly rushed to John's side. "You don't have to do this," she said.

But John was determined. "Polly, if they steal our dreams, they put a chain around our souls. Somebody's got to stand tall."

Fueled by his dream, John Henry picked up his pace, too. His muscles strained. Sweat poured from his face. He swung his hammer over one shoulder and then over the other. Bit by bit, he not only caught up with the steam drill—he passed it!

And then —*thud*— John's hammer was halted in mid-swing. He looked up to find himself standing at the foot of a solid rock wall. The mountain! He had gone as far as he could go, and he had gotten there first. He had won the race! The crowd cheered.

They knew John could do it.

In his own heart, John knew he could do it, too. Slowly, he drew himself up. He held the hammers above his head and smashed them against the mountain. With a hammer in each hand, his arms became a windmill of power. Rocks and boulders flew everywhere, and John Henry dug his way into the mountainside.

Inside the mountain, sparks from the steam drill and the red-hot trails of John's hammers lit up the darkness. The earth shook as the two giants battled their way through the rock.

Meanwhile, Polly and the railroad workers waited on the other side of the mountain to see who would come out first.

Finally, with an explosion of rock and dust, a powerful force broke through. As the dust cleared, the crowd strained to see. Yes! It was John Henry! He raised his hammers high into the air just as the sun set in the west.

John had done it. But something was not right.

John's chest heaved, and he collapsed to his knees.

Polly rushed to him and caught him as he fell back into

her arms. John Henry

had given every ounce

of strength he had to

give.

Years later, Polly

would show her son,

John Henry, Jr., a story

quilt that told of his legendary papa—about his

strength, about his determination, about the way that even as he breathed his last breath, he was smiling: "'Cause he moved that mountain and led us to the promised land," she would say. "You can move mountains, too, baby. All you gotta do is believe."

Walt Disney's
TOBY TYLER

When Toby got back to the farm, his uncle was angry. "Toby, you forgot to feed the hogs," he said. "The hungry hogs broke down the fence around their pen. They rooted up all the turnips."

"Now we have no turnip crop to sell," said Aunt Olive. She looked sad.

Toby had to show his uncle and aunt how sorry he was. Suddenly, he knew what he would do. He would earn money to pay for the ruined crop. That night, when everyone was asleep, Toby packed up his things and crept outside. He was going to join the circus!

Ajax, the bareback rider, had hurt his leg. "Now who will ride with Jeanette?" said Colonel Castle. "We have a big show next week."

"Let me try!" said Toby. "I rode my uncle's horse many times."

But *doing tricks* on a horse was another matter. Could Mighty Benjo and Sam Treat make a bareback rider of Toby in just one week? Day and night they worked with Toby in the practice ring. Toby had no time that week to play with Mr. Stubbs. Poor Mr. Stubbs thought his friend was still angry.

The hoops were in place. The band played faster. The horses cantered faster. Then Jeanette and Toby, standing on their horses' backs, jumped through the flames. . . .

Out they came on the other side of the hoop and landed gracefully on their horses!

Mr. Stubbs chattered happily. His friend was smiling again. Toby wasn't angry anymore. Mr. Stubbs leaped into the ring and up onto Toby's horse. Everybody cheered and clapped for the daring young bareback riders and for the happy monkey!

Mickey was very happy. It was a lovely afternoon, and he and Minnie were going on a picnic with their friends. Mickey peeked inside the picnic basket Minnie had packed. Yum! There were peanut-butter-and-jelly sandwiches, cold-meat sandwiches, deviled eggs and potato salad, radishes and onions, pink lemonade, and a big chocolate cake!

Mickey picked up the basket, and he and Minnie went out to the car, where Pluto, Goofy, Daisy Duck, and Clarabelle Cow were waiting for them.

"It seems strange to go without Donald Duck," said Mickey as they drove away.

"Yes," said Minnie, "but there is always trouble when Donald is along."

None of them saw Donald watching them leave.

Everyone sang merrily as Mickey drove down the road to the picnic grounds. It was a perfect day for a picnic. First they went for a walk along the riverbank. Then they found a grassy spot beneath a tall tree. They left the picnic basket there while they went for a swim in the swimming hole.

How good that fresh, cool water felt! They swam and floated and played around, and had a wonderful time. But afterward, when they

returned to their grassy spot, their picnic lunch was gone! "We'll soon find out about this!" Mickey cried. They searched all over the picnic grounds without seeing a sign of the picnic basket. At last, they came out on the road, near the spot where they had left Mickey's car.

It was then that they met Donald Duck, walking down the road. He had a fishing pole over one shoulder. A bundle hung from the end of the fishing pole.

Donald opened his bundle and spread out his lunch. Yum! There were peanut-butter-and-jelly sandwiches, cold-meat sandwiches, deviled eggs and potato salad, radishes and onions, pink lemonade, and a big chocolate cake!

Mickey threw Minnie a puzzled look when he saw the contents of the picnic lunch.

Minnie turned to Donald and flashed her sweetest smile. "Did you bring a knife for cutting the cake, Donald?" she asked.

"Er—I had one somewhere," Donald said, searching around.

"You let Jimmy go!" Pollyanna said loudly. "He didn't hurt anything, and neither did I."

Pendergast was so surprised that he let go of the boy. Jimmy dashed for the door, and disappeared quickly before the old man could catch him.

Pendergast
glared at
Pollyanna.
"Go on. Get
out of here!"
he bellowed.
Pollyanna
started to go,

then stopped short. On the wall were beautiful patches
of colored light.

"What a beautiful rainbow!" she said with a gasp.

"That's not a rainbow," hissed Pendergast. "It's the sun shining through the prisms of the lamp."

"I like to think it's a rainbow," said Pollyanna. Then she added, "Maybe you're not glad I came here, but I am." And she skipped merrily out of the room.

One day, the townspeople decided to hold a big fair to raise money for a new orphanage. Pollyanna did all she could to help. She even asked Old Man Pendergast to take a booth and sell glass pendants.

"We'll call them rainbow-makers," said Pollyanna.

Meanwhile, far below, in the dark shadow of the skyscrapers, the little house wondered, What's to become of me? Will I never feel the sun again, or feel the gentle touch of the summer breeze, or hear the song of the meadowlark?

Poor forgotten little house. There was nothing left now—not even hope. And so, when the wrecking and moving company came for her, with tools and trucks and chains, the little house decided it was just as well. I'm just in the way, she thought. I'm no good to anybody. And we all have to go sometime.

So, with the mailbag loaded onto the train, Casey Jones was off, and right on schedule, too. Yes, the weather was fine, the engine was purring, and there was clear track ahead as far as the eye could see.

The train rolled through the countryside, mile after mile, and Casey sat back, put up his feet, and settled in for a smooth journey. It was going so well that Casey even had time to get choosy with the pieces of coal that were going into the furnace.

Poor Casey Jones! He had no idea what was in store for him as his train wound its way through the mountain pass and raced onto the bridge. Halfway across—*kaboom!*—the dynamite exploded, the bridge gave way, and Casey's train tumbled into the dark canyon.

Now, for a lesser engineer, that might have been the end of the story. But Casey Jones just fired up that train engine and steered her straight up the canyon wall. Oh, it took some straining, but eventually Casey Jones had that train out of the canyon and back on track.

Furiously, Casey Jones shoveled coal into the furnace until it was full to bursting. Thick black smoke poured out of the smokestack. The train barreled down the track at lightning speed.

Casey frantically worked the controls, trying to get every last ounce of power out of his machine. And just

 when it seemed that nothing could stop brave Casey Jones and his mighty engine, Casey turned to look down the track . . .

. . . and saw another train hurtling toward him from the opposite direction.

The men on the other train managed to jump clear before the two trains collided in a tremendous wreck. But not Casey Jones.

Was this the end of the line for the brave engineer?

Hours later, out west, the station clerk checked his watch. Casey Jones was ten minutes late. It was so unlike Casey to be late that the clerk doubted he was coming at all. Sadly, the clerk shuffled over to the ARRIVALS board and raised his hand to erase Casey's name. Suddenly, he heard the distant sound of a train whistle. Could it be?

A battered locomotive limped into the station carrying a bruised Casey Jones. And do you know what Casey was clutching in his arms?

Yes, it was the mailbag. It hadn't been easy, but

Casey Jones had done his duty. When all was said and done, he had gotten the mail through on time. Well—almost.

# of Your Favorite Disney Tales in These
Illustrated and Gilded Storybook Volumes!